To all who told me
not to tell anyone...

www.mycrazystories.com

MAYA KNOWS A SECRET

(SHHH...)

TEXT AND ILLUSTRATIONS
DANIEL GEORGES

Maya had a curious question for her dad this morning. "Daddy, what is a SECRET?" she asked.

"Hmmm... A secret is something only you and someone else know," he answered.

"And how do I know when someone is telling me a secret?"
"Well, after telling you a secret, a person will say:

DON'T TELL ANYONE!"

Maya got very excited!
She went out to find someone to tell her a SECRET...

"The weather is warm today," said the grocer.

Maya was upset...
People told her many things today,
but none of them were secrets!

She knew that because no one said:
"Don't tell anyone!"

I DON'T KNOW ANY
SECRET!

On her way back home, Maya froze in front of a shop.
There was a fluffy yellow hat in the window...
 and SHE LOVED IT!

The shop owner noticed Maya's agitation and said:
"It's the last one I have, don't tell anyone!"

DON'T TELL ANYONE?...
DON'T TELL ANYONE?...THAT'S IT!

SOMEONE FINALLY TOLD MAYA
A SECRET!

Maya trotted joyfully back home thinking:
"I have to bring my mom now to buy me that hat!"

She saw her friend and shouted without stopping:
"MIMI...I KNOW A SECRET!"
"Really?" said Mimi, "What is it?"

"I SAW A WONDERFUL YELLOW HAT
AT THE SHOP AROUND THE CORNER,
AND IT'S THE **ONLY** ONE LEFT!"

Then she hurried away knowing little that...

A SECRET
IS ONLY
A SECRET
IF KEPT
A SECRET!

The fluffy yellow hat was gone.

"I told you not to tell anyone," said someone.
Maya turned around.
It was the shop owner, smiling at her.

Inside the shop boxes were stacked
all the way up to the ceiling!
The man opened them and threw out
all kinds of colorful hats flying
all over the place.

"PICK FROM THESE!"

"Our new collection for next season!
You're the first one to see them, so don't tell anyone!"
Then he winked and asked: "What do you say?"

"IT'S A SECRET, AND THIS TIME..."

Thank you so much for reading this book!

Look for the whole series and
share your review on Amazon.

GET ANOTHER BOOK... FREE!

Quick! Go to
www.mycrazystories.com
and get a free ebook from the series!

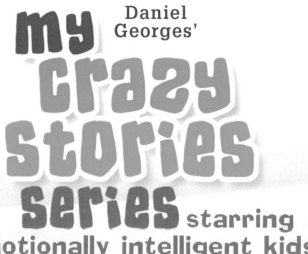

36088677R00015

Made in the USA
Middletown, DE
11 February 2019